ELIEZER BEN-YEHUDA

The Father of Modern Hebrew

Other books by Malka Drucker

Celebrating Life: Jewish Rites of Passage

Eliezer Ben-Yehuda Street—named in honor of the valiant pioneer—in modern Tel-Aviv CONSULATE GENERAL OF IS-RAEL

JEWISH BIOGRAPHY SERIES

ELIEZER BEN-YEHUDA

The Father of Modern Hebrew

MALKA DRUCKER

illustrated with photographs

LODESTAR BOOKS E. P. Dutton New York

Copyright © 1987 by Malka Drucker

Library of Congress Cataloging in Publication Data

Drucker, Malka.
   Eliezer Ben-Yehuda, the father of modern Hebrew.

   (Jewish biography series)
   Includes index.
   Summary: A biography of the man who resurrected
Hebrew, lost for 2000 years except for reading and
writing, as an everyday language, thus uniting Jews
of the modern world by providing a common tongue.
   1. Ben-Yehuda, Eliezer, 1858–1922—Juvenile
literature.   2. Jews—Palestine—Biography—
Juvenile literature.   3. Hebrew language—Revival—
Juvenile literature.   [1. Ben-Yehuda, Eliezer,
1858–1922.   2. Jews—Biography.   3. Hebrew language—
Revival]   1. Title.   II. Series.
DS125.3.B417D78   1987   492.4'092'4   [B]   86-15213
ISBN 0-525-67184-6

Published in the United States by E. P. Dutton,
2 Park Avenue, New York, N.Y. 10016

Published simultaneously in Canada by
Fitzhenry & Whiteside Limited, Toronto

Editor: Virginia Buckley

Printed in the U.S.A.   COBE   First Edition
10 9 8 7 6 5 4 3 2 1

for my father, William Treiber

Contents

Acknowledgments

The author wishes to thank Harvey Horowitz, librarian at Hebrew Union College–Jewish Institute of Religion; Dr. Yona Sabar; and Gay Block.

O N E

A Student of Torah

The old teacher tightened his hands around a glass of hot tea as the icy wind slid under the door of the wooden shack. His pupil, Eliezer Yizhak Perelman, who had been born in this house, was used to the cold and didn't mind it. At his teacher's urging, he buttoned his threadbare jacket. But he paid no attention to whether his frail body was freezing. He was aware only of the book in front of him.

On that cold day in 1869, in the town of Luzhky, Lithuania, which was part of Russia, Eliezer's teacher had given him a very difficult passage to read and interpret in the Talmud. The Talmud, a book written in Hebrew to help people find solutions in the Bible to their problems, had been challenging Jewish scholars for nearly two thousand years.

Reading ancient Hebrew was easy for Eliezer because he'd learned to read Hebrew at three. Still, the teacher was asking him for the meaning of the text and not simply a translation into Yiddish, the language European Jews used for everyday speech. Like most Jews in Russia, Eliezer spoke Yiddish but could only read and write Hebrew. No one spoke Hebrew except for prayer and study.

Eleven-year-old Eliezer had been studying the Talmud with his teacher for two years. The teacher came only when Eliezer's mother could pay him, which wasn't often. Leibel, the boy's father, had died six years earlier and had left the family penniless. He had been known in their little town as a *luftmensch*, literally "a man in the air." Everyone respected him for his wisdom and ideas, but he never earned a living for his family.

Luckily, Eliezer's mother, Feigah, was a practical woman. She had opened a grocery store in the front of their miserable house and sold such things as flour and candles. The store gave the family just enough money to clothe and feed four children and two adults. This pained Feigah because Eliezer, her youngest child, needed more than food. He needed to learn. By the time he could talk, she knew that he was different from her other children. Eliezer was hungry to know everything. He asked her questions all day long, and she was sorry she had few answers for him.

Eliezer played with his long silken side curls, one of the marks of an Orthodox Jew, as he struggled with an answer for his teacher. The man marveled at the boy's concentration. Finally, Eliezer squirmed and looked up from his book. His burning hazel eyes held the teacher's attention as he spoke. The man listened to Eliezer's insightful answer with wonder and sadness. A mind like that deserved more than a poor teacher in a poor little town. But Eliezer had no chance of a better education. The boy would probably end up a water carrier or at best struggle to teach himself as his father had done. Still, it wouldn't hurt to talk to the boy's mother again.

Feigah listened to the teacher's words of praise. Eliezer

reminded her of her wealthy brother, David, who had also been a brilliant scholar in his youth. He lived in a large house not far from Luzhky. He was still deeply religious and a student of the Torah. After the teacher had left, Feigah asked Eliezer if he'd like to study at his uncle's house. Eliezer was delighted with his mother's idea. He hated the strain his lessons put on the family, yet his hunger to learn was overpowering. David's eager acceptance of Eliezer assured him that he could continue his lessons and not burden the family.

Uncle David greeted Eliezer with a warning. "I demand only one thing of you, that you have a serious attitude toward your education." Eliezer assured him that he intended to study hard, but his uncle's sternness made Eliezer long for his family's love. His uncle showed him around the house. It was much larger than any house he'd ever seen, and it was warm, thanks to a huge hearth in the main room. When Uncle David took Eliezer to the room he would use, the boy's eyes grew big. Eliezer had never even had his own bed! The uncle looked at his nephew's shabby clothes and frowned. "In the morning, we'll get you fitted for some decent clothes. Good night," he said abruptly and left Eliezer in his new room. Everything was suddenly quiet. When he was home, he often wished for a little privacy. Anytime he found an empty corner to read in, he felt lucky. Now that his wish had come true, he felt lonely. He blew out the candle and tried to sleep in his large bed.

The time Eliezer spent at his uncle's house was wonderful. He saw several teachers regularly. One teacher instructed him in Hebrew, another in Torah, another in law. When Eliezer turned thirteen, he became a Bar Mitzvah. He was now responsible for anything he did and was a full participant in Jewish life. He was ready to study at a yeshiva, a rabbinical college. Eliezer expected this new move to be challenging, but he didn't realize the challenge his uncle had in mind.

"Eliezer, as you know, now that you're a Bar Mitzvah it's time for you to go to the yeshiva at Polotzk. I want you to take full responsibility for yourself there." The uncle paused. "From now on, you're on your own. I no longer will support you, because I don't want you spoiled. You are to work hard, even if you have to endure hunger, cold, and suffering. It will improve your scholarship and help to make you a great rabbi." Eliezer had experienced enough poverty to disagree with his uncle. When his stomach growled emptily, it was difficult to care about the fine points of law.

He was sorry to be leaving the comforts of his uncle's house, but his feelings for the man were mixed. Although Uncle David had been generous, his gifts came with strings attached. Life in Polotzk might be difficult, but Eliezer would be on his own. No longer would Uncle David tell him how serious he needed to be or what he had to study. He would find out for himself.

T W O

An End
and a Beginning

By the time Eliezer reached Polotzk, he was so tired he could hardly stand. Traveling all day over rutted roads in a wooden wagon had worn him out. He climbed down from the wagon, stretched to ease the kinks out of his weary body, and looked around. The wagon driver threw Eliezer's bag out of the wagon and drove off. Eliezer wanted to ask the driver how to get to the yeshiva, but it was too late. Polotzk was a huge city of big buildings and streets teeming with people. A shiver of fear shook his body as he tried to find his way to the yeshiva.

When he finally arrived there, the rabbis helped him find a place to sleep and eat. He quickly made friends with other boys who shared his passion to learn. One Friday evening, on the Sabbath, a friend took him to meet Rabbi Joseph Blucker, a rabbi who was no longer part of the yeshiva because he had begun to study outside the world of Torah and Talmud. European philosophy, literature, and science intrigued Rabbi Blucker. Orthodox Jews such as Uncle David mistrusted anyone who needed more than Torah. For them, the Torah contained all the world's wisdom. There was nothing that anyone could add to it, and studying anything outside the Torah was dangerous and ungodly.

Until the middle of the nineteenth century, there were few new ideas and teachings threatening the Jewish tradition. But when machines and scientific inventions began to change people's lives, Judaism, which had remained much the same for two thousand years, found itself in conflict with the outside world.

Orthodox Jews said the solution to the conflict was not to allow Jews to study anything new. Some Jews decided that if Judaism didn't fit into the modern world, then there was no point in remaining Jewish. They became Christian and joined the majority. Others took a middle course. They remained faithful to the Jewish tradition, but they also enjoyed living in the modern world. These Jews took the best of the new ideas and incorporated them into Judaism; their form of Judaism wasn't the same as their ancestors'.

Rabbi Joseph Blucker fell into the last category. Eliezer watched him carefully pour wine into a silver goblet in preparation for the Sabbath blessing. The rabbi picked up the goblet and gently cradled it in his palm. With his eyes closed, he began to hum the prayer's melody softly to himself. He swayed slightly to the music. Then he opened his eyes and smiled at Eliezer, who had been staring at him. The rabbi motioned to Eliezer to join him in chanting the blessing. Eliezer had heard of the man's revolutionary reputation, but no one had told him of the rabbi's love for the Jewish tradition. New ideas didn't destroy religious feelings, Eliezer decided.

After dinner Rabbi Blucker began to discuss philosophers and scientists who were not only modern but also non-Jews.

Eliezer listened intensely. Suddenly he realized that there *were* new ways to look at things and understand the world. The Torah was only one path leading to knowledge.

Blucker invited Eliezer to study with him twice a week. Eliezer jumped at the chance and spent months learning not only Talmud but also new texts about Judaism. One Friday night after dinner, Eliezer went into the rabbi's study to discuss whatever book Blucker had chosen for the evening. But the rabbi had no book in his hand. Eliezer was worried. "Is he angry because I haven't studied enough?" he wondered. He'd accept reprimand, study more. "Please keep the lessons going," he silently begged his teacher.

The few months he'd been with the rabbi had taught him so much. What was especially wonderful was expanding his knowledge of Hebrew. From the time Eliezer was a little boy, he enjoyed being able to read and write Hebrew. Before he met the rabbi, his only knowledge of the language had been from prayers and the ancient holy books. He loved reading modern religious books written in Hebrew.

Looking around the room quickly, Rabbi Blucker reached under his seat cushion, felt for something, and then slowly extracted a book. "How strange," Eliezer thought, though relieved that they'd have their study session. The rabbi handed the book to Eliezer. He looked at the book with curiosity. He read the Hebrew letters slowly: They spelled *Robinson Crusoe*. This obviously wasn't a tract from Talmud. It was an English novel written in the eighteenth century that had been translated into Hebrew. Eliezer looked up at the rabbi and asked, "You mean Hebrew can be used for more than religious purposes?"

Rabbi Blucker smiled. "If Hebrew can describe the adventures of Moses in the desert, why can't it describe the life of a shipwrecked sailor?" he asked.

Eliezer took the book and read it in secret. He knew from the way the rabbi had hidden it that this novel was forbidden in the Orthodox yeshiva. While the story entranced him, the language intrigued him more. His old teacher in Luzhky had told him that God had made the world from the letters in the Torah. Like atoms, Hebrew letters were the world's building blocks. Everything was made of letters—the sun, a face, a river. Before there was light, God used letters to say "Let there be light!" *Robinson Crusoe* used the same letters. "Maybe everything is holy," Eliezer thought, "and Hebrew can express it all."

Eliezer continued to read whatever his teacher gave him. He would happily have gone on studying with the rabbi forever, until one day he looked up from a book to see the angry face of his uncle. Uncle David had heard rumors that his nephew was following the ways of evil. Not only was Eliezer reading modern ideas, but he was reading them in Hebrew, the holy language! His uncle had come to take Eliezer home and put him back on the road to piety.

Eliezer reluctantly returned to his uncle's house, but he couldn't put away his new books. Whenever he was alone, he secretly read from books hidden in the lining of his jacket. After morning or afternoon prayers, he stayed in the empty synagogue and read.

One evening he sat reading in a corner, with all his concentration on a new book. Suddenly the candles in the synagogue blew out. In the darkness, Eliezer squinted to see what had happened. There had been no wind. Six ghostly figures slowly moved toward him. God was punishing him for reading these books! He dropped the book and ran screaming from the synagogue.

The white figures hovered where Eliezer had been reading. Then they removed their sheets, and Eliezer's uncle thanked his friends. They'd come to scare young Eliezer out of his new ways, and they'd done a fine job. Although his uncle was afraid to touch the book that Eliezer had left behind, one of the other men picked it up and said, "David, look at this. It's not so bad. It's a modern work proclaiming the glory of God."

The uncle shook his head. His face was hard. "Is it written by the ancient rabbis? No? Then I have no interest."

Eliezer had run back to the house. His uncle wasn't there. He became suspicious, and when he heard Uncle David enter with his friends, he guessed what had happened. He felt for the book under his mattress and began to read, secure in knowing that he didn't have to worry about heavenly spirits scaring him out of his wits.

He heard his uncle say good-bye to the other men and then listened for the dull footsteps coming up the stairs. Quickly Eliezer blew out the candle, stuffed the book back into its hiding place, and closed his eyes, pretending to be asleep. He heard the creak of the door as his uncle opened it. He lay still, trying to breathe regularly. Suddenly he heard his uncle's sharp voice, full of anger. "Eliezer, sit up! Do you think I'm a fool? I just burned my finger on the wick of your candle. You haven't been sleeping for long!"

His uncle slid his hand under the mattress and found *Robinson Crusoe.* He began to tremble with rage. "Enough!" Uncle David shouted. His eyes, sharp as knives, hurt Eliezer even in the darkness. "There is nothing to be done with you! Leave my house and take your scandalous books."

Eliezer quickly gathered his things and left the house in the middle of the night. He would never see his uncle again. It was winter and very cold. He began walking quickly to keep from freezing. But soon he stopped. Where was he going? He had no money, and he dared not go home to his mother for fear she would be angry with him for ruining his opportunity to become a rabbi.

The cold began to creep under his collar no matter how much he ducked his head into his coat. He decided he'd walk until he reached the nearest town. For several hours he trudged, his feet wet and freezing. He stared into the night but couldn't find even one light. Finally, when he couldn't take another step, he saw a building ahead. He had reached Glubokaya, a little city of a few thousand people. In the dimness of night he searched for its synagogue.

As soon as he spotted the synagogue, he stepped inside

the building, which was only a little warmer than outside with the wind blowing. It was a few hours before morning prayers at seven, so he lay down on the floor to rest. The next thing he knew, he was being awakened gently by a large, kind-looking man. "Wake up, son. What's your name? Where are you from?"

Eliezer sat up and rubbed his eyes. His chest and feet hurt from his long walk. "Eliezer Perelman," he said with effort. The man who had awakened him, Schlomo Yonas, a wealthy whiskey maker, noticed how pale and weak he was. When the morning service was over, he took Eliezer home with him.

Eliezer entered the dining room to eat breakfast and meet the Yonas family. Friendly though curious eyes greeted him around the table as he loaded his plate with herring and bread. Eighteen-year-old Deborah, the oldest of the six children, observed the young man her father had brought home with special interest. He was really still a boy, but he possessed an intensity belonging to a man. Little Pola liked the way Eliezer looked. She'd never seen anyone with long side curls, and since his were red, they looked like red springs. She thought they were beautiful.

After breakfast Deborah showed Eliezer her father's library. When he looked closely at the books that filled the large, well-furnished room, Eliezer shrugged his shoulders and offered her an embarrassed smile. He couldn't read most of the titles. Only the Hebrew and Yiddish books were recognizable to him.

"What are these languages?" he asked. She pointed to one and said it was French. Another was Russian and another was German. "Can you read these books?" he asked Deborah. When she said yes, he begged her to teach him.

Eliezer stayed with the Yonases for two years, learning from Deborah and enjoying the affection of the entire family. Except for a nagging cough that never left him, he became physically stronger and grew into a handsome young man. The Yonas family had come to love him as a son, and he loved them so much he called them his second parents. Eliezer hadn't forgotten his mother, though. He wrote her about the kindness of these people but carefully left out telling her that they weren't Orthodox.

Like Rabbi Blucker, the Yonas family allowed the modern world to change them. Eliezer left his strict upbringing and fit into their household easily. He stopped wearing the long black coat and fur hat he had worn at the yeshiva. The only problem came the day he cut off his side curls. When Pola saw him, she howled with disappointment. "My mother and uncle would agree with the little girl," Eliezer thought, amused by Pola's reaction.

By the time Eliezer was sixteen, Father Yonas, as Eliezer had taken to calling him, knew that the young man needed a teacher more experienced than Deborah. So he decided to send Eliezer to the gymnasium in Dünaburg. It was a high school for Russian boys who wanted an advanced education. Eliezer would live in a non-Jewish world for the first time. He couldn't wait to go, but he had to make two promises before he left, one to Father Yonas and one to Deborah.

Father Yonas was an enlightened man who valued the Jewish tradition. "Deborah has taught you many languages, Eliezer, and you will learn even more at the school. But don't forget Hebrew. It is the language that all Jews share in common." That was an easy promise. Eliezer's early love of Hebrew had not disappeared when he learned other languages.

The other promise was more personal. Deborah had grown to love Eliezer, and his leaving was painful to her. On their last day together, he acted as though it were any other day. He didn't want to say good-bye; he would miss her. "Eliezer," Deborah said as he was about to leave, "you know how I feel about you." Eliezer looked at his shoes and swallowed. "Promise that you'll remember me."

Devorah Ben-Yehuda

"I promise," he blurted in Yiddish, the language of his childhood. He was so embarrassed he forgot to speak in Russian, the everyday language of the Yonas household. "Say it in Hebrew," she said. Jews always used Hebrew when they were about to do something that was binding, like make a contract. He looked in her eyes and knew that part of her would be with him in Dünaburg. Father Yonas interrupted them to tell Eliezer it was time for him to go. He hugged Eliezer so tightly that the young man began to cough.

"Good-bye, my boy, please write," the older man said. "And be sure to see a doctor about your cough!" Eliezer nodded and left quickly before anyone saw his eyes fill with tears.

THREE

Lightning

If Deborah had surprised Eliezer with a visit to Dünaburg, she might not have recognized her old student. When he'd left Glubokaya, he was dressed like her father, with short hair and a well-tailored suit. He looked like a well-bred young Russian. But when he joined a group of students called the Narodniki, "Sons of the Russian People," Eliezer began to dress like a peasant, wearing high cavalry boots and loose colorful clothing. As a Narodnik, he encouraged the Russian people to return to a simple life of farming, and to love their country and language.

All over Europe, people were beginning to value what made their nations different from one another. The Jewish people weren't part of this new movement, which was called nationalism. Although they lived in every European country, they weren't full citizens of any. They usually were forced to live in a designated quarter of the city and were not allowed to own land. In countries such as Russia and Poland, they suffered from pogroms, senseless violent attacks on their villages. Jews were often killed during pogroms. Because of this history, many Jews didn't care about the culture of the country in which they were living.

The Jews had once had their own nation, which was called Israel in ancient times. But they had little to remind them of it, because they had left Israel two thousand years before. The only bit of nationhood they still possessed was Hebrew, the language their ancestors had spoken in Israel. They had forgotten how to speak it, except in prayer, but many of them could still read it in the ancient books.

Eliezer's interest in Russian nationalism was his way of breaking from the past. With the same enthusiasm and intensity he had once brought to the Talmud, he now worked to assimilate Russian culture. But something stopped him from becoming completely Russian and cutting himself off from the Jewish people. Years later he would write, "There still remained one thread, and this thread all the forces of nihilism could not cut. This thread was—love for the Hebrew language! Even when everything Jewish had become strange to me, even repugnant, I could not separate myself from the Hebrew language, and, from time to time, wherever and whenever I happened to chance upon a book of modern Hebrew literature, I could not summon enough willpower to overcome my desire to read it."

Eliezer read everything he could about the Russian-Turkish War. In 1878, the Russians were helping the Balkan people gain their independence from Turkish rule, and as a Russian nationalist, he wanted the Balkans free. Sometimes he wondered why he cared so much about a people and a land he had so little connection with. His friends noticed too. Despite their respect for his intelligence, they teased him about his passionate interest in the Balkans' struggle.

One evening, close to midnight, Eliezer sat reading the

newspaper about the latest battle. Suddenly he was on his feet. Like the light bulb that appears over someone's head when he has an idea in a cartoon, a light flashed inside Eliezer's mind. He heard a voice inside him say that the Jewish people, like the Balkan people, could be nationalists. It was time for "the revival of Israel and its language in the land of its forefathers." Later, when he tried to describe the moment, he said it was "lightning before my eyes."

Eliezer had just turned twenty when this idea came to him. He didn't know it then, but that moment would decide how he would spend the rest of his life. If he'd been a little older or a little more knowledgeable, he might have set the idea aside as interesting but impossible to do. How could one person convince the Jewish people to leave Europe and to speak a language that hadn't been spoken in two thousand years? Luckily, Eliezer's youth and intensity allowed The Idea, as he called it, to live and grow.

In 1878, seven million Jews spoke Yiddish. They also knew a little of the language spoken in the countries in which they lived. Yiddish-speaking Jews lived in Europe. Jews scattered in other parts of the world spoke either Ladino, a mixture of Spanish and Hebrew, or they simply spoke the language of the country in which they were living. Although two or three hundred thousand Jews knew Hebrew, no one spoke it as a first language. Only on rare occasions was Hebrew spoken other than for prayer or Torah study. If a Yiddish-speaking Jew wanted to talk to a Spanish Jew, he or she might use Hebrew, their common language, to exchange greetings. Some religious Jews also spoke Hebrew on the Sabbath. Hebrew would sometimes be used in legal documents between two Jews to bind it to the laws of Judaism.

But once Hebrew had been the daily language of the Jewish people. What had happened to it? It was almost, like Latin, a dead language. For thirteen hundred years, when the Jewish people lived in Israel, they spoke Hebrew to tell

jokes, sell a horse, and talk to God. But when they left Israel and lived in other countries, they learned the languages of the new countries. Because their children saw and
heard the new language all around them, they found the
new language easier to speak than Hebrew.

The old language stayed alive in writing, however. Every
Jewish child learned how to read and write Hebrew. According to the rabbis, one could truly understand the Torah
only in Hebrew, because the meaning lay hidden in the letters. The Torah spoke to generations of Jews because it could
be seen in many ways. The more it was read, the more
meanings it revealed. The rabbis said the Torah was a
"hammer that breaks the rock in pieces." Just as a hammer
breaks the rock into many pieces, one biblical verse conveys
many meanings. A translation of the Torah into another
language would limit the ways the Torah could be understood, because only Hebrew contained all its meanings. The
language had become a substitute for the land of Israel. It
was a sweet reminder of an era when Jews were proud of
their place in the world. For most Jews living in the nineteenth century, dreams and memories made life bearable.

Eliezer's idea came just in time, because fewer and fewer
books were being written in Hebrew. The language, which
wasn't being renewed by people speaking it, had become
clumsy. It couldn't provide the words needed for the new
ideas of the last half of the nineteenth century. Young writ-
ers preferred to write in Yiddish or in a European language.
Yiddish was a wonderfully expressive language, full of feeling and color. By contrast, Hebrew was bare and stiff, the
dry language of the scholar. No one used Hebrew for
everyday expressions. Orthodox Jews had a different reason for not speaking Hebrew. They believed it was wrong
to use a holy language to say something like "Take out the
garbage."

These objections to speaking Hebrew didn't touch Eliezer. He no longer respected the rigidity of Orthodox Ju-

daism. Yiddish triggered painful memories. It reminded him of his mother's poverty, his uncle's punishment, the constant fear of pogroms. Yiddish, borrowed from European languages, was spoken by a weak, defeated people who contented themselves with dreams. The language was a symbol of Jewish exile. On the other hand, Hebrew reminded Eliezer of his first teacher, of Rabbi Blucker, of Deborah, and of a time when Jews were strong and free in their own country. The Orthodox Jews were waiting for the Messiah to return them to their former glory. Eliezer wouldn't wait; he'd do it himself.

Eliezer began to make plans for his dream. First, he needed to leave Russia and go to Paris, which was the center of new social and political freedoms. Eliezer wanted to be close to the source. Second, he wanted a profession that would bring him money, respect, and a chance to meet important people. Becoming a physician seemed the best choice, so after graduation from the gymnasium he left for Paris to study medicine at the Sorbonne. The Yonas family continued to support him.

With its wide boulevards, outdoor cafés, and beautifully dressed citizens, Paris enchanted Eliezer. Nothing in Russia had even hinted that there was such a world as Paris. He bought a cane, along with a top hat, and strolled the streets, cutting a handsome figure with his auburn hair and brilliant hazel eyes. The French that Deborah had taught him was stilted, but he soon learned to speak almost as well as a Parisian. For the first time, Eliezer met people, Jews and non-Jews, who liked his ideas for reviving Hebrew. One of the most important people he met was Dr. Charles Netter, the founder of a colony of pioneers in Palestine, the land that had once been called Israel and would be called Israel again in modern times. Eliezer went to Netter to tell him of his plan and to hear what conditions were like in Palestine.

The meeting gave Eliezer information, but not what he expected. Dr. Netter listened to Eliezer talk and asked him not so much about his ideas but about his cough. It had grown worse during the cold, damp French winter. He would cough so hard that his handkerchief would become soaked with blood. Netter examined him after their interview. As Eliezer had feared, he had tuberculosis in his lungs, a serious but common disease one hundred years ago. There was no cure for it; it would become worse. The only suggestion the doctor offered was for Eliezer to go to a warm climate and not work so hard. He had only a short time to live.

Eliezer left Netter white-faced and shaken. He had studied enough medicine to guess that he had tuberculosis, but he never imagined he had so little time left. He had just begun to work toward his dream. He paced his small dormitory room, angry and frustrated that he wouldn't be able to help the Jewish people to be strong again.

Whatever time he had left he wanted to use wisely. If he wrote a paper that explained why he thought Jewish nationalism was a good idea, it could influence people after he died. He began to gather his thoughts about the subject and decided that he would submit an article—written, naturally, in Hebrew—to *Ha-Shahar (The Dawn)*, a Hebrew magazine published in Vienna. As he began to compose the article, he grew excited. Suddenly it became clear to him how land, language, and people fit together. The land needed the language and the language needed the land. If the Jewish people, scattered all over the world and speaking seventy different languages, were to go to Palestine, they needed a common language. Hebrew, so important to Jewish culture, was the natural choice. And if Jews tried to revive Hebrew when they were surrounded by non-Jews, they would never succeed. They had to be where they would not be constantly hearing any other language.

The writing of the article so absorbed him that he forgot about his illness. He would imagine hearing children speak Hebrew and look forward to this happening. Then he would remember his fate. His friends hounded him about leaving

Paris and going to a warmer climate. He promised he would go to Algiers when his article was published. His friends worried: What if the article wasn't published?

When Eliezer finished the article, he sent it off to Vienna and waited nervously for a response. The article had already been turned down by a magazine in Warsaw. Soon he heard that it had been accepted, but that the editor had changed his title from "A Burning Problem" to "A Weighty Question." If the editor had known Eliezer, he would have sensed that *burning* was the proper word to describe how the writer felt about his idea.

In the article, published in 1879, the weighty, or serious, question the author asked was, "Why should we not do the same as other people [and] take action to protect our nationhood lest it perish and be utterly destroyed?" He was worried about the future of the Jewish people. Although Eliezer wasn't the first person to suggest that they needed a homeland, his article introduced a new word and idea in Hebrew: *leumiut,* "nationalism."

A nation is the sum of three elements: a people, a land, and a language. Eliezer focused on the importance of language. Language is more than an instrument of communication; it embodies a people's spirit and uniqueness. One of the chief differences among European countries was the distinct language spoken in each. Eliezer wrote, "We have a language in which we can write everything we want to and we can speak it if we only want to."

He was sure that if the Jewish people, in the sunny and once glorious land of their ancestors, began to speak Hebrew again, the language would erase the painful memory of Europe. They would become a new kind of Jew—proud, strong, and dignified. "It is this language which unites all the children of Israel from the four corners of the globe . . . it is the language of our forefathers, the language of our prophets, the language of our sages—the precious national tongue of the entire nation, and therefore this language alone should be taken . . . for the schools. The students in the schools will remain faithful to their parents and nation—because the education will be national even though it will be according to the spirit of modern times," he wrote. Eliezer was the first person to suggest the revival of Hebrew as an everyday language. He felt it could be more than the language of prayer and study.

The twenty-one-year-old author signed his first published article with a new name: He was now Eliezer Ben-Yehuda. He wanted to rid himself of the past. His last name, Perelman, was a name derived from German. Ben-Yehuda means "son of Judea," which is another name for the Jewish people. Yehuda was also Eliezer's father's Hebrew name. Eliezer didn't know it then, but giving himself a Hebrew name would start a pattern for the young Jews who left Europe for a new life in Israel. The first step they would take would be to give themselves a Hebrew name.

Not everyone agreed with the ideas put forth in "A Weighty Question." In fact, many Jews thought Eliezer's point of view was dangerous. Orthodox Jews were furious that he would have the nerve to interfere with God's plan to return the Jews to Israel and that he would suggest they speak the holy language. Others thought Christians would be angry that the Jews wanted a homeland, and they would step up their persecutions. And there were Jews who felt that Eliezer didn't know what he was talking about. Palestine was no longer a land of beauty and wonder. It was a desert with swamps, and anyone who suggested that Jews return to it was crazy.

Yet there were some people who agreed with Eliezer and were grateful for his article. He found that the article made him new friends. The last thing he wanted to do was leave Paris and his friends and go to Algiers. But he was terribly ill and didn't have a day to waste.

As soon as he arrived, Eliezer began to feel better and was able to leave his room to explore the city. But he met with a problem. How would he talk to the Jews of Algiers? He had always spoken Yiddish with Jews who didn't know French or Russian. These Jews didn't speak Yiddish. They spoke Arabic or Ladino. But they also spoke Hebrew, and so did Eliezer. For the first time in his life, he had to speak Hebrew to communicate.

The Hebrew he heard, however, was not the Hebrew he'd been taught in Lithuania. The words were the same, but the pronunciation was as different as British English is from American English. Eliezer knew Ashkenazic, or European, Hebrew. It had a soft, mellow pronunciation that sounded like Yiddish. The accent often fell on the first syllable. What Eliezer was hearing in Algiers was Sephardic Hebrew, which was closer to the way Hebrew had been spoken originally. Sephardic Jews came from Spain and lived in countries near the Mediterranean Sea. The Hebrew they spoke hadn't been as changed by other languages. It had a clean, vigorous sound that pleased Eliezer. For example, Ashkenazic *Shabbos*, "Sabbath," became *Shabbat*, with the stress on the second syllable, and *emes*, "truth," became *emet*. The pronunciation, so different from that in Europe, sounded fresh and strong.

After many months, Eliezer was well enough to return to Paris. One day he was having lunch with a new friend who also loved Hebrew. Eliezer shifted out of French naturally, after speaking Hebrew for several months, and the conversation continued in Hebrew. Because his thoughts came quickly and he wanted so much to tell about his experiences in Algiers, he found himself groping for words. It was nearly impossible to have a conversation in Hebrew. He said to his friend, "I need a list of new Hebrew words that are necessary for everyday conversation." Eliezer began to search for words. When he wanted a glass of water, he had to find the word for glass. He remembered studying a part of the Talmud that described measuring vessels. Sure enough, he found a word that described something a person drank out of.

He loved being back in Paris, but he began to cough again. Since he couldn't stay in the city he loved, he decided to go to Palestine and prove that his idea could work. He didn't know how long he would live, but he wasn't going to waste another day of his life thinking about his dream. He was going to live it.

When he wrote the Yonas family about his decision, he wasn't prepared for their response. Father Yonas was furious. He told Eliezer that Deborah had been waiting for him to return. She loved him and thought they had an understanding that they would marry when Eliezer was finished with school. Eliezer was shocked. Didn't they know how sick he was? He replied that of course he loved Deborah. He loved her too much to leave her a young widow. He didn't see how he could marry anyone because he was so ill.

Deborah wrote Eliezer and told him she wanted to be with him no matter how little time he might live. She wanted to go to Palestine and help him. Eliezer needed no coaxing. He made arrangements to meet her in Vienna. They had not seen each other for seven years. Eliezer was twenty-three, and Deborah was twenty-seven. When they finally met face to face, they were shy with each other. They each had carried pictures of what the other looked like and the pictures didn't match what their eyes were seeing. Deborah's wholesome beauty delighted Eliezer. He preferred her looks to the beauty of Parisian women that came from wearing makeup. Eliezer's appearance astonished Deborah. He was just sixteen when she saw him last. Now he was a handsome young man.

They left Vienna in August 1881, and began their long journey to Palestine. They had so much to tell each other, but he held the greatest surprise of all. After their wedding, in Cairo, Eliezer told Deborah that they would never speak any language besides Hebrew ever again. Deborah was so stunned she couldn't think of anything to say in any language! But she listened carefully to his words as he explained, in simple Hebrew, that their family would be proof that Hebrew could be revived. Deborah would be remembered as the mother of the first Hebrew-speaking child in the modern world.

It was a good thing Deborah, who was now called Devorah (her name in Hebrew), was in love with Eliezer, or she might have argued loudly. She might have reminded him that she knew very little Hebrew. Wasn't it enough that she was going to a strange country with him? Couldn't they tackle one challenge at a time? But she saw more than love in her husband's eyes. She saw his pain and understood his hurry.

F O U R

Palestine

From the minute they boarded the boat in Alexandria that would take them to Jaffa, Palestine, Eliezer impatiently watched for land. He'd dreamed of this place for so long. All he could imagine came from what he had read in the Torah. He knew the country must be different two thousand years later, but how? On the way to Palestine, they had stopped at other ports along the Mediterranean Sea. The boat picked up dark-skinned Arabs in bright clothing who were also on their way to Palestine. Their presence made Eliezer uneasy. Except for Devorah and him, there were no Jews going there. "Who lives in Palestine?" he began to wonder. As the boat slowly drifted toward the dock, Eliezer strained his neck and squinted to get his first glimpse.

Now he saw that Jaffa was indeed an Arab city, full of camel drivers, peddlers, and farmers. If there were Jews in Jaffa, they weren't near the dock. Instead of being happy that he had finally arrived, he was horrified. Years later he would describe the moment as feeling like "a stranger, the son of a foreign country and a foreign people; back to the land of my forefathers. I have no political and no civil rights. I am a foreigner. . . . I suddenly broke. Something like remorse rose in the depths of my soul. . . . My feet stood on the holy ground, the land of the forefathers, and in my heart there was no joy. . . . I did not embrace the rocks. . . . I stood shocked. Dread! Dread!"

The noise, smell, and filth of Jaffa disturbed Devorah as much as the discovery that there were Arabs in Palestine had shocked Eliezer. Their fine European clothes suddenly seemed wrong for this part of the world. They couldn't wait to leave Jaffa. Eliezer stepped into a little inn to find out how to get to Jerusalem. Before he could say anything, however, the man greeted him with "Shalom," which means "hello" in Hebrew. The word was like medicine to Eliezer. The doubt and dread that had hit him when he had arrived in Jaffa disappeared. Hebrew was spoken here! He wasn't crazy to have come after all.

Devorah still felt uncertain. And when she saw the ramshackle carriage pulled by three skinny horses that was to take them to Jerusalem, she thought longingly of Europe. Eliezer did not notice the carriage. It was the driver who won his attention. He was speaking Hebrew to his horses! And the Hebrew was earthy, clear, and conversational. The language of the wagon driver, not the language of the professors, was the language that Eliezer wanted to revive for all the Jewish people.

After traveling all night, they arrived at dawn in Jerusalem, which was known as the City of Gold. The golden domes of the mosques looked almost pink in the pale early light. Both Devorah and Eliezer were enchanted by the city's beauty. But as they wandered through the city, they found ragged children and sick, deformed people begging in the streets. Eliezer wondered if David, king of the Jews twenty-five hundred years ago, would have recognized his city.

The Jewish quarter of Jerusalem. Eliezer and Devorah Ben-Yehuda encountered similar conditions when they arrived from Europe. ZIONIST ARCHIVES AND LIBRARY

When Eliezer was a little boy, he read about Palestine in the Torah. It was described as a "land flowing with milk and honey." At the end of the nineteenth century, the country was almost impossible to live in. It was barren, with deserts and swamps. Disease killed a large portion of the population. Was it too late for the Jewish people to return to this country and make it beautiful and healthy again?

Eliezer didn't know the answer to this question, but he did know that the first thing he needed was to get a job in Jerusalem. The journey had taken all his money. Luckily for him, his writings were already known in Palestine. Israel Frumkin, editor of *Ha-Havazzalet*, a weekly newspaper, was eager to have Eliezer work for him.

Frumkin was an Orthodox Jew, as were most of the twenty-five thousand Jews who lived in Palestine in 1881. They weren't there to build a new country, as Eliezer was. Some had never left the land. Others were there because they were very religious and wanted to be in the land of their ancestors, no matter how dreadful the living conditions. Ashkenazic, or European, Jews, they had fled the modern world. They didn't want to change anything in Palestine. They accepted everything as God's will.

The Palestinian Jews weren't pioneers. They weren't even a close-knit community. They were part of many small communities, each with its own food, dress, and religious customs. They also each had their own language or way of speaking. Ladino, Arabic, Yiddish, Spanish, and variations of Russian were all spoken in Jerusalem. "Every group and faction," Eliezer wrote in amazement and frustration, "is a whole world unto itself, every world with its own sun, stars, and moon revolving about its own orbit."

The only thing Eliezer found attractive about these people was their knowledge of Hebrew. The language had never completely stopped being spoken in Jerusalem. The Sephardic Jews spoke it with anyone who couldn't speak their everyday language, and spoke it especially with Ashkenazic

Jews. Therefore, the Sephardic Jews spoke Hebrew to Eliezer. The pious Ashkenazic Jews thought Eliezer might be Sephardic because he didn't speak Yiddish, so they also spoke Hebrew to him.

Eliezer listened carefully to every unfamiliar word he heard and immediately wrote it down. Besides simply expanding his Hebrew vocabulary, this helped him talk to Devorah. Since they only spoke Hebrew to each other, they spent a lot of time pointing. If Devorah wanted a little cream for her coffee, she'd say, "Eliezer, *s'licha* (excuse me)," and point to the cream pitcher on the table.

Although Eliezer had left his Orthodox beginnings, he quickly saw that he had to gain the trust of the Jewish establishment in Jerusalem. He stopped shaving and let his red beard grow thick and full. Instead of wearing stylish clothes he wore a long black coat with a prayer shawl over it. He also wore a red Turkish fez to show his respect for the Turks who ruled Palestine. Except for his head covering, anyone would have thought he was a rabbi.

Devorah also became, at least outwardly, an Orthodox woman. She shaved her head as married Orthodox women do and covered it with a kerchief. She never let her shoulders show in public, no matter how warm it was. She made her kitchen kosher, which meant they didn't eat milk and meat together, didn't eat pork or shellfish, and whatever meat they ate had to be killed according to Jewish law. They also went to synagogue on Shabbat.

But Eliezer couldn't change inside. His articles weren't Orthodox, and they often made his readers and his editor angry. Instead of firing Eliezer, Frumkin offered a solution. He gave Eliezer his own monthly paper, called *Mebasseret Zion (The Zion News)*. It would be under Frumkin's supervision and an added section to the weekly paper. Eliezer received very little money for his work, however, and he needed another job because Devorah was pregnant.

When Nissam Behar, principal of Alliance Israelite Universelle, a school in Palestine supported by wealthy European Jews, asked Eliezer to teach, he wanted to take the job right away, but he didn't. He told Behar that he would take the job only if he could teach his classes in Hebrew. That was fine with Behar. He'd come to Eliezer because of his reputation as a man with a passion for Hebrew. Eliezer was exactly the person he wanted.

The climate in Jerusalem made Eliezer feel better, but his two jobs left him exhausted. He also spent energy fighting those who saw him as a threat to Judaism. They threw stones at him as he walked to school and shouted at him, in Yiddish, that he was misusing the holy language.

Eliezer was prepared to fight his battle alone to make the Jews a Hebrew-speaking society again. But he never expected his mission to be so difficult. His lungs, the filth and disease in Palestine, the struggle to make a living, and the hostility of most of the Jewish population in Jerusalem all added up to certain failure. If it weren't for a surprise during the Passover of 1882, Eliezer's strength and Devorah's courage might have failed.

Life in Palestine was difficult, but compared to what was happening in Europe, the Palestinian Jews were lucky. Pogroms had become more violent and frequent. Poverty and starvation were destroying the Jewish people. The only good thing about the times was that they pushed a few young adventurous Jews to find a solution. These Jews called themselves the Biluim, which was short for "House of Jacob, come let us go."

Like Eliezer, the Biluim believed that the Jewish people could be free and strong again. They wanted to leave Europe and make a place where Jews would be welcome. They imagined healthy young children brown from the sun, and strong men and women planting crops on land that had once been dusty and barren. These people would no longer speak Yiddish, a borrowed language. They would speak the language of biblical heroes and become heroes themselves.

Members of the Biluim, the group of settlers who traveled from Europe to Palestine to join Ben-Yehuda   ZIONIST AR-CHIVES AND LIBRARY

Not everyone thought the pioneers were right. In fact, most people thought they were crazy. Palestine was tree-less, malaria wiped out part of the population repeatedly, and the Turkish government hardly encouraged their ar-rival. Besides these obstacles, most of the pioneers knew nothing about farming.

Eliezer was conducting the family seder on the first night of Passover when he heard a soft knock at the door. Al-though he didn't know who called, he was pleased. Tradi-tion encourages anyone giving a seder to invite anyone who is hungry to come and eat. A stranger is especially wel-come. But what greeted Eliezer at the door that Passover night wasn't one stranger but twenty-six smiling young people who had just arrived from Europe to help him re-vive Hebrew and rebuild Palestine. They had read his arti-cles and had paid close attention. More than that, they felt his conviction. They knew that he wasn't sitting in a com-fortable chair in Paris telling others to go to Palestine. He was actually there, living his words. The Biluim had come to join Eliezer in his work and make it theirs, too.

They followed Eliezer's lead and changed their names to fit the land. Grien became Ben-Gurion, "son of a lion," and Rachmilewitz became Onn, "vigor." The new names expressed the pioneers' feeling of being reborn in the new land. The names also linked them to their ancestors. Jewish tradition takes names seriously. God allowed only Moses to know His name. God, Jehovah, Yahweh, Lord, Adonai, Elohim are substitutes for the real name. In ancient times, children were often named after plants or animals, either because their parents loved the natural world or because they wanted the child to be like the plant or animal. A name could also be connected to a parent. Ben-Zvi means "son of Zvi," and Zvi means "deer." In the Torah, names change as people grow and change. When God spoke to Abraham and told him that he would be the father of a great nation, God changed his name from Abram to Abraham and his wife Sarai's name to Sarah.

The Biluim and the second group of pioneers who followed them six months later moved out into the countryside and built a settlement, which was a little farm. It was the first time most of the pioneers had ever worked with their hands. They lived in simple tents and planted crops for food. They called the settlement Rishon Le Zion, "first in Zion," and although Eliezer didn't live there, they proclaimed him its father.

Everyone on the settlement spoke Hebrew. Some questioned speaking the new language, at least in the beginning. Barren land, heat, and malaria were enough of a challenge without having to struggle every time they wanted to speak. After they had conquered some of their other problems, then they would tackle Hebrew. But the settlement leaders were firm. The new language was part of the plan. The people must bind the language to the land and the land to the language.

The leaders got their way, but for many people, Yiddish remained the comfortable language. A settler described how

Rishon Le Zion, the first settlement the Biluim established

he felt speaking Yiddish after having spoken Hebrew for two hours as the same wonderful relief he had after riding bareback on a donkey for two hours and then getting off and walking on his own legs.

Eliezer became a father twice that year. Soon after the birth of Rishon Le Zion, Devorah gave birth to a healthy baby boy. Eliezer and Devorah wanted to name him Ittamar, "island of palms," but their new friends persuaded them to follow the Sephardic custom of naming the first-born son Ben Zion. Now Eliezer had a First in Zion and a Son of Zion. Because Eliezer wanted Ben Zion to be the first child in two thousand years to speak only Hebrew, he went to extremes to make this possible. When Devorah cried out with labor pains, he reminded her to speak only in Hebrew. He was worried that his almost born child might hear a "foreign language." Only after her baby was born and she said *yaldi*, which means "my son," to him, did Eliezer smile.

F I V E

The Deer

Eliezer's critics never bothered to be polite. They often told him how crazy or foolish he was to try to resurrect Hebrew. Even so, he wasn't ready for the attacks on Ben Zion. The little four-year-old boy, handsome, with bright dark brown eyes and thick black hair, didn't talk. Most children begin to speak by the time they are two years old. Ben Zion only babbled nonsense. "What can you expect," people gossiped, "when he won't allow the boy to talk to anyone who doesn't speak Hebrew?" It was true. When friends came to visit the family, Ben Zion was sent to bed early so he wouldn't hear a foreign language. He wasn't even allowed to hear birds sing and horses neigh for fear he would make their sounds. Eliezer wanted Ben Zion to hear only Hebrew.

Language is one of the most important things a parent

teaches a child. Eliezer believed that Ben Zion would learn Hebrew by hearing it from his parents. This would have been possible if Hebrew had been a comfortable day-to-day language, but Eliezer's Hebrew was stiff and dry. Could he play games or sing songs with his baby? Devorah knew less Hebrew than Eliezer. How would their son learn to tell his mother that he didn't feel well, that he loved the color red, or that he wanted more to eat?

Ben Zion didn't even try. He just pointed and babbled. Eliezer's friends would privately take Devorah aside and tell her to speak any language she chose to Ben Zion. But Eliezer insisted that Ben Zion would eventually speak and that his language would be Hebrew.

One morning Eliezer left on a short trip for Jaffa. He gathered up his bags, said good-bye to Devorah and Ben Zion, and ran down the stairs to catch the carriage. As soon as he was out of sight, Devorah began to sing to Ben Zion a Russian lullaby that she remembered from her childhood. Enchanted with hearing his mother sing for the first time and hearing her use words quickly and without struggle, Ben Zion gave her his complete attention. He began to hum the melody and sway to its rhythm.

Neither mother nor son heard Eliezer's footsteps. He'd forgotten something. The sound of Devorah's voice, however, distracted him from his purpose. Enraged by her deception, he screamed at Devorah. The memory of that day stayed with Ben Zion forever. When he grew up, he wrote, "The moment caused a great shock to pass over me when I saw my father in his anger and my mother in her grief and tears, and the muteness was then removed from my lips and speech came to my mouth." In the end, Eliezer was right. Ben Zion began to speak Hebrew.

Ben Zion was only one of Devorah's concerns. Eliezer and his editor, Frumkin, couldn't work together anymore. Eliezer had quit his job, and they had no rent for their two rooms. Eliezer, however, assured her that now that he could write for his own newspaper, he would have so many readers they wouldn't have to worry about money anymore.

Eliezer knew exactly what kind of paper he wanted to publish. Even though he looked like an Orthodox Jew with his beard and long black coat, underneath he was still the elegantly dressed Parisian. He wanted his paper to possess the style and polish of *Figaro*, the world-famous sophisticated French journal. Eliezer would design and write his paper to appeal to the new pioneers beginning to come to Palestine. He would write plainly and strongly about events in Europe and Palestine.

Only one obstacle interfered with his lovely dream—the name of the paper. The Turks wouldn't allow anyone to begin a paper without an existing license, and they wouldn't issue new licenses. The only way around the problem was to take over an existing newspaper. Eliezer was eager to do anything to get started, but the only paper available was called *Ha-Zvi (The Deer)*. "The Deer!" Eliezer shouted. "My paper will be nothing like a quiet, gentle deer!" He had no choice, though. No matter how wrong the name, if he wanted a newspaper he'd have to call it *The Deer*—even if its editor was a lion.

Now that he owned *Ha-Zvi*, he worked even harder than before. Over his desk he placed the words:

THE DAY IS SO SHORT
THE WORK TO BE DONE SO GREAT!

He didn't know how short his day might be, so he spent every second as fully as his health would allow. He set the type himself and, with Devorah's help, delivered the first issue on Friday afternoon, October 24, 1884. He knew the only day his readers would have time to enjoy *Ha-Zvi* would be Shabbat, the day of rest, so he always planned his deliveries right before.

The first issue covered news beyond Jerusalem and Jewish life. It included events in Egypt, Sudan, France, China, Russia, and Argentina. Rishon Le Zion and the other new settlements were also part of the news. After the first months, Eliezer added news of medicine, new books, and musical events.

Ha-Zvi became popular immediately. His readers found the easy conversational tone refreshing. Many had never read Hebrew that didn't sound like Talmud. Eliezer's style was fresh, newsy, and entertaining. Rarely was a paper thrown away after one reading. As many as forty people might share a single issue, until the newsprint became smeared from too much handling.

Besides spreading news, the paper had another important task. Eliezer wanted to expand the number of words in Hebrew, and he wanted to create a writing style that was similar to the way people spoke. He listened carefully when he walked down the street to pick up common Hebrew expressions. When he let his students out of class for recess, he listened to them, too.

He used the paper as a place to introduce new words each week. Palestine was an exotic country for its readers, with plants and animals they had never seen before. Eliezer didn't want people pointing at a rose and a lily and calling them simply flowers. Sometimes he found a clue for a word in the traditional books. *Elevator* came from a line in the prayer book that says "go up and come down." He would also create words by combining two Hebrew words to mean what one foreign word meant. For example, *library* became *bet ha-sefer*, "a house for books." Years later, Hebrew scholars coined the word *makhshev* for computer. It means "to make thought." El Al, the Israeli airline, means "to the heights."

Eliezer didn't make word lists or call attention to his new words by underlining them in his articles. He was afraid that if people saw a new word without a sentence to give meaning to it, they'd make fun of it. He simply used these new words in his articles. Sometimes readers would protest and write a letter to the paper:

A new newspaper, a new style . . . The papers are full of life. . . . How precious is the material! How alive the style! And how dear to us are . . . the new and revived words which we meet most in the descriptions of the life on the agricultural colonies! But most of the young readers simply do not understand the new words, and of course they will not remember them. Even though most of the words are taken from the Mishna and the Talmud, their meaning lies hidden even from the young person who has read Talmud. . . .

Other readers wrote that they didn't "just read *Ha-Zvi*; we learned it." This pleased Eliezer. He told his readers that his new words were bricks—they needed builders to "construct from them a palace for our language." Not everyone would like all his words, but if half of them survived and "their birthplace forgotten," he'd be satisfied.

Some people may have laughed at his attempts to make new words, but Orthodox Jews didn't find Eliezer amusing. Besides objecting to the paper for its use of Hebrew, they especially disliked his article about *shemittah*, the Jewish law that allows the land to rest for one year out of seven. The earth isn't touched for twelve months and the plants growing on it aren't pruned or fed. Eliezer understood that *shemittah* gave the soil time to get its nutrients back. He also knew that if the country practiced *shemittah*, all the new trees and plants would die from neglect. He suggested that laziness, not devotion to God, was behind the appeal of *shemittah*. The Orthodox community quickly banned the paper. No Orthodox Jew was allowed to buy or read *Ha-Zvi*.

Eliezer gave up all hope of convincing the Orthodox community that he wasn't an enemy of the Jewish people. He stopped wearing Orthodox clothes and trimmed his beard to a fashionable goatee. Outside Jerusalem, especially in Jaffa, he had the support of the pioneers. He no longer needed the Orthodox community. He despised the way they lived,

A poster Eliezer Ben-Yehuda had made, exhorting Jews to speak Hebrew. The poster states, "Speak Hebrew and you will become healthy." ZIONIST ARCHIVES AND LIBRARY

and he said so in his paper. Almost all of them were terribly poor, but none of them worked. He felt they were taking advantage of a tradition in which scholars and rabbis spent their time studying and learning instead of working for money. Judaism values learning so highly that the community considered it a privilege to support those who learned and those who taught.

The problem in Jerusalem was that many of the Jews there weren't scholarly. They were simply lazy. They depended upon European Jews to support them. Twice a year a member of the Orthodox community would travel to Europe to get money from fellow Jews. First he would assure his listeners that the Jews never had a more devoted and pious community than the one in Jerusalem. Then his eyes would fill with tears and he would sigh. "What's wrong?" someone would ask. He would explain how tragic it was that the Jerusalem scholars could not study with peace of mind. They had to worry about putting food on the table for their families. Then he would look especially needy and ask in a small voice if the European Jews could give him a little something to help the scholars of the holy land.

These appeals were effective. They had supported Jerusalem's Jewish population for hundreds of years. Occasionally there were grumblings from other Jewish groups that this system, called *halukkah*, was unfair. But no one wanted to criticize *halukkah* publicly and be accused of attacking one's own people.

No one, that is, except Eliezer. Sephardic Jews worked the land. "Why couldn't the Ashkenazic Jews do the same thing?" he asked in his newspaper. Working with one's hands was considered undignified by these Jews. Eliezer thought begging was undignified, too. "If these young students are going to be given money," he wrote, "let them live on a piece of land they can farm."

Despite his battles, Eliezer tried to find time for one of the great pleasures in his life, listening to Ben Zion talk. By the time he was eight, the boy spoke Hebrew so well it no longer sounded stiff. He told jokes and made his father laugh. Ben Zion's words made Eliezer sad and happy at the same time, because he knew that he'd never speak as naturally as his son. His children and grandchildren would complete his work.

This wasn't the first time the teacher trailed behind his students. When Moses led the Jews to the promised land, he wasn't allowed to see it himself. In fact, none of the Jews who had been slaves were allowed to enter the new land because they bore the memory of their slavery. They could never create a free society. In the same way, Eliezer would never be able to speak Hebrew as well as the children growing up in Palestine. He once said that his only regret was "I was not born in Jerusalem, nor in the land of Israel."

Ben Zion loved his father but also resented the family's great responsibility. They had to show the world that speaking Hebrew was possible. Many hated his father and Ben Zion, indirectly, for being his son. The older boys in school taunted him about his father's paper being banned.

He was so lonely his mother allowed him to have a dog. The growing family—there were now four children—scarcely had room, but Devorah knew how much the dog meant to Ben Zion. One afternoon, after school, he took his dog out for a run in the fields near his house. As he turned for home, he saw a group of boys coming toward him. The dog began to growl. Ben Zion spoke to him softly and told him to keep still. "Listen," the largest boy said in Yiddish. "He speaks the holy language to a dog!" The other boys laughed.

One of them threw a stone at the dog. More stones rained on him. Ben Zion tried to protect him, but it was no use. When the dog no longer moved, the boys stopped and left Ben Zion alone with his only friend. Only when his mother found him sobbing in the field did Ben Zion let go of the still animal.

In his grief, Ben Zion learned something about his father.

Those who opposed him were stubborn and heartless. Why should they decide how all Jews should speak? His father had something strong inside him to continue to work for his dream. That strength made life difficult for those around him, but now Ben Zion appreciated his father's courage. He would help him any way he could.

S I X

A New Family

By the time the Ben-Yehuda family had been living in Palestine for ten years, they numbered seven. Besides Ben Zion and his brother and sisters, many children spoke Hebrew in 1891. The settlements and the schools had been teaching in Hebrew long enough for the children to begin to speak it outside the classroom. For some, it was the only language they knew.

Eliezer's readers had become comfortable enough in Hebrew to read books translated by him from French, German, and English. Each week he published a small part of a book in the paper. This helped sell more copies, because readers bought the paper just to find out what would happen next.

Life grew more satisfying for Eliezer but became more difficult for Devorah. Despite the success of *Ha-Zvi*, she still never had enough food for the family. She took a job teaching to bring in more money. At thirty-seven, Devorah felt as if she were eighty. She was tired all the time, and she'd begun to cough. She had caught Eliezer's tuberculosis.

Unfortunately, Devorah didn't have good stretches of time the way Eliezer did. He fought the disease with a rare will. Most of the time he kept it from stopping him. That it hadn't killed him was a miracle. But once Devorah began to cough and run a fever, she feared she had little time left. She begged Ben Zion to help his father fight his battles. She had only strength to speak to one child, but she knew Ben Zion would be the leader of the others. He had come to understand and respect his father, so his mother didn't have to worry. But he loved his mother so much! He prayed every night that she would live.

When Devorah asked Eliezer to marry her sister, Pola, he knew that there was no hope. Although he protested to her that she would live, he quickly wrote his mother to come to Palestine to help him with the children. Eliezer and the children were with Devorah when she died.

Eliezer had to arrange for Devorah's funeral immediately. Jewish law requires that a deceased person be buried within twenty-four hours after death. To his shock, the burial society refused to help him because his paper had been banned. She was not fit to be buried in the cemetery. If he wanted, they would bury her outside the cemetery walls.

Storming out of the synagogue, Eliezer went to the leader of the Sephardic community. They had never imposed the ban on him, so they were honored to bury his wife. When the Ashkenazic leader heard of this, he quickly changed his mind. Devorah was buried at the Mount of Olives, a mountain cherished by the Jewish people. It is the first choice for a burial place, and many leaders and prophets have their graves there. If a person cannot be buried on the mountain, the family may sprinkle a little soil from the Mount of Olives over the coffin.

His followers waited to see if he would write about Devorah's death and the Ashkenazic community's response to it. After a week's time he simply quoted Jeremiah from the Bible, which explained how he valued her life: "I remember you, the kindness of your youth, the love of your espousals, when you went after me in the wilderness, in a land that was not sown."

Eliezer's grief did not end with Devorah's death. Within two months, his three youngest children died of malaria. The family was left with Ben Zion; his little sister, Yemima; and Eliezer. His mother stayed with the family, but her ignorance of Hebrew made life even more difficult. One of the few words she could say was *behahteed*, "someday." She said it in response to Yemima asking her several times a day when her mother, brother, and sisters would come back.

Eliezer withdrew into himself. No one could comfort him. He threw himself into his work to push away the pain. His critics said that God had punished him for his evil work. Eliezer knew better. Even with his crushing loss, he knew he had to continue.

Devorah had been dead for several months when Eliezer received a letter from her younger sister, Pola. Eliezer had last seen her when he'd gone to Russia asking her family for money. He had criticized her for not being Jewish enough, but it didn't bother her. She'd been in love with Eliezer since she was a child, and any attention he gave her made her happy.

Now Pola was nineteen. She still loved Eliezer, which was one reason for her writing him. Another was that just before Devorah died, she wrote Pola thanking her for her picture: "You are as beautiful as Aphrodite. I had a dream about you the other night, Pola. I saw you standing before me and I said to you: 'Sister, if you wish to become a princess . . .'" Devorah didn't have the strength to finish the letter. Since her death, Pola understood what her sister thought she should do to be a princess. She should take her sister's place and marry Eliezer.

In her first letter to Eliezer, she told him she was thinking of changing her name to a Hebrew name and wanted his suggestions. Happy that she was thinking of this, he found her letter a welcome relief from his unending work and his sadness. He sent her a list of twenty names with their translations. When she wrote back, she told him she liked Hemda best. Its meaning, "joy and beauty," was what she loved most, because she wanted to be the joy and beauty in Eliezer's life. She didn't tell him that, of course.

Eliezer, however, caught the real meaning of her letter. He was lonely. He responded, "I suggest you change your name to Hemda. I also suggest that you change your name to Ben-Yehuda. Would you?"

Pola-Hemda was ready to pack her bags and set out for Jerusalem when her family stopped her. They asked her to think about it. She had been considering a career in science and had been going to college. If she married Ben-Yehuda, she would have to give up everything. Her parents had been to Palestine. They described in vivid detail the filth, poverty, and barrenness that would surround her. Although they didn't mention it, they also didn't want to lose another daughter. What if their youngest child became ill like her sister?

The Yonas family weren't the only people opposed to the marriage. Everyone, except Eliezer and Hemda, thought it was a terrible idea. Friends begged Eliezer to reconsider, but no one was able to change his mind. Then he spoke to the doctor who treated his tuberculosis and had cared for Devorah.

The doctor said, "I know how lonely you are, Eliezer. And I know that your children need a mother. But you must understand that tuberculosis is an infectious disease. Devorah caught it from you, and you could give it to her sister." The terrible truth began to sink in. "Or," the doctor went on, "she could stay healthy, but you could die soon—your life is a miracle. But this poor young woman would be left a widow looking after your children. Is that what you want for her?"

The doctor's words were cold water in Eliezer's face. How foolish of him even to consider another marriage! The young woman had swept him up in her passionate enthusiasm, and he'd forgotten he had no right to marry her. She'd be throwing her life away. Immediately he sat down and wrote her, almost as an older brother rather than as a lover, that much as he would love to marry her, he thought it was a bad idea. He was taking back his proposal of marriage.

Eliezer didn't remember this young woman very well. He'd forgotten how powerful she was. She snapped, "When I was five, you stopped my crying by promising to marry me. I'm still waiting!" More importantly, she told him that she was unmoved by his argument because she had every intention of fulfilling her sister's last wish. She also felt that she owed something to her sister's children. "Whatever time we will have, Eliezer, will be enough," she concluded.

Much as Eliezer wanted to protect her, he found this strong young woman's appeal too attractive. He wanted her to be his wife, and if she was willing, he wouldn't stop her. Three months later, wearing a handsome European suit and his fez, he met her in Odessa. When his bride-to-be demanded an explanation for his head covering, he explained that he was proud to be part of the Jewish return to the East. Hemda replied that she was glad to be part of it, too. Since she knew no Hebrew, they spoke in Russian.

They were married in Constantinople (now Istanbul), where no family or friends saw the ceremony. On their way to Jerusalem, Eliezer tried to prepare Hemda for life in the old, new country. He painted a harsh picture to protect her from the disappointment he and Devorah had experienced eleven years before.

Hemda, however, was not so horrified by Jerusalem as she was shocked by the condition of his household. When they arrived at the apartment, she had to strain her eyes to see in its darkness. All the curtains were drawn. The house was cold and empty. Whatever furniture there was had been

Left, Eliezer Ben-Yehuda wearing a tarbush (fez), as he looked when he arrived in Odessa to meet Hemda Yonas   GAY BLOCK; *right,* Hemda Ben-Yehuda   ZIONIST ARCHIVES AND LIBRARY

castoffs from friends. Everything in the house was unloved and uncared for. Eliezer, who had never been interested in the house's appearance, cared even less about his surroundings since Devorah's death. Though there were children in the house, there were no signs of their presence. Not a doll or a ball signaled that they lived there. The only signs of life were Eliezer's papers lying everywhere.

What upset Hemda the most, however, were Ben Zion and Yemima. Eliezer called them in to meet the aunt who was to be their new mother. Thin and pale, they spoke slowly and haltingly to Hemda. She had never seen such sad children. If she had had any doubt about coming to Palestine, the sight of the children erased it.

She was also disturbed by their clothes. Eliezer's mother had dressed Ben Zion according to Orthodox tradition. Ben Zion wore a long black coat, black shoes, and a wide-brimmed black hat. He wore side curls as his father had when he was a boy. Compared to the children on the settlements, he looked as though he had come from another century. Yemima looked funny too. She wore a dress several sizes too big for her, and her hair looked as though it hadn't been brushed in weeks.

The children tried not to stare at Hemda, but they were struck by how lovely she was. She resembled their mother a little, but neither child remembered ever seeing their mother healthy and strong. Hemda seemed almost like a child herself!

They didn't know what to call her. They had called their mother *Ima*, which means "mother" in Hebrew. Although Hemda was lovely and Ben Zion and Yemima liked her, they didn't want to call her by a name that would stir up sad memories. Eliezer and Hemda were sympathetic and tried to offer solutions, but none of them felt right to Ben Zion. After thinking about it for several weeks, he said to Hemda, "I know! We'll call you *Amma*. *Abba* is 'Daddy' and *Ima* is 'Mommy.' You'll be in between."

Hemda wanted to help Ben Zion and his sister be more like other children. One of the first things she did when she came to live with them was to cut their hair and get them clothes that fit. She gave them toys and games and taught them how to use a ball with stones to play a game like jacks. The apartment was really one large room and allowed no one privacy. She gave each child his or her own corner. Hemda showed the children a new world. Before she came, they'd never had toys, privacy, or pretty clothes. She sang to them and the family slowly moved from darkness toward light and happiness.

The changes pleased Eliezer, but something worried him. Hemda had made the house so welcoming that many people had begun to visit the family regularly. Many of their guests spoke Russian, French, and German to Hemda, who couldn't yet speak Hebrew. The language in the house was no longer only Hebrew. Eliezer had mellowed since Ben Zion was a baby, and he knew how much happier the family was. The children were no longer lonely and isolated from the outside world. But Eliezer couldn't sacrifice his dream. Hebrew must be spoken in his house, but how could Hemda learn it quickly?

His teaching experience showed him how important it was to hear and speak Hebrew all day long. So he brought his printing press into the house and all his workers with it. The printers, who spoke only Hebrew, surrounded Hemda with the language. They asked her where the bathroom was and how the children were. They showed her how the paper was published. Because Hemda was eager to learn, she soaked up every word and enjoyed the company of her teachers. Within six months she was speaking well enough to have conversations with people on the street. Reviving Hebrew had become her goal too.

If Ben Zion was Eliezer's first Hebrew miracle, Hemda became his second. He traveled all over the country with her, showing off her Hebrew. Everyone knew that Hemda had only recently arrived in Palestine. She was living proof that even with little childhood knowledge of Hebrew, an adult could learn to speak it in a short time.

Hemda didn't mind showing off, but what she loved about the trip was seeing the settlements for the first time. Rishon Le Zion was an oasis in the middle of the desert. The settlement was surrounded by tiny villages with people living in huts and burning cow dung for heat and cooking. Eliezer beamed when the children greeted them with "Shalom." But when Hemda spoke to the women in Rishon Le Zion, she used an interpreter. She thought it was silly, because she could certainly understand their French and Yiddish and could have easily answered them with words they understood. But it was important for them to hear her answering them in Hebrew. Before their visit ended, several women tried to speak faltering Hebrew with her.

Pioneer women, members of the Biluim ZIONIST ARCHIVES
AND LIBRARY

Eliezer and Hemda were concerned that the settlement women didn't speak Hebrew among themselves. They both felt that in some ways women would be the key to the success of the language. Children spend more time with their mothers than with anyone else when they are learning how to speak. If the mothers spoke Hebrew, the children would naturally follow.

On the ride back to Jerusalem, Hemda and Eliezer talked over many things. The men on the settlement urged Eliezer to begin writing the dictionary he had been promising to write for years. They pointed out that every day new words were born into the language. The only way people could expand their knowledge would be if there were a modern Hebrew dictionary.

Eliezer simply shrugged his shoulders and smiled. "Who has the time?" he answered by way of question. Every morning he arose at dawn, partly to get a good start on the day and partly because he had always loved the peace and freshness of daybreak. Maybe if he gave up his five hours of sleep each night, he could write the dictionary.

SEVEN

New Life for an Old Language

Eliezer knew that the men at Rishon Le Zion were right. If modern Hebrew was to survive and flourish, it must have a dictionary. Without it, a person in one town might use a word for pumpkin that in another town might mean "candle." Someone had to gather the words and find common meanings for them. Hebrew was also on its way to becoming a living language. A dictionary could assure Hebrew's future by recording its progress into the modern world.

But how would he find time? Always before, Eliezer's determination had led him to a solution. Once again he solved his problem, but this time with Hemda's help. She already spoke Hebrew with a special softness and grace. If Eliezer could persuade her to take over part of the writing in *Ha-Zvi*, she'd bring a new voice to the paper. Most important, he'd have more time.

Hemda protested. First, she didn't know the language well enough, and second, she wasn't a writer. But Eliezer had read her letters from Russia and knew how persuasive they had been. He finally convinced her, and she agreed to write a column, "Letters from Jerusalem." It would be about whatever interested her.

Because much of her life was as a wife and mother, she wrote about shopping for food, clothes styles, raising children. The women on the settlements eagerly waited for the paper each week. Hemda, by helping to bring the language to women, was becoming as passionate as Eliezer about Hebrew. Her first contribution to Eliezer's dictionary was the word *ofnah*—which came from the ancient *ofen*, "style"—for fashion.

Busy as she was, Hemda wanted more. She wanted a child of her own. Within eighteen months of her coming to Israel, *Ha-Zvi* happily announced: "A daughter has been born to Eliezer and Hemda Ben-Yehuda, and her name is Devorah." The baby had been named for Eliezer's first wife, Hemda's sister. The little girl was Eliezer's sixth child. She was special to him because of her name, because she was the first child in his new family, and because she was the first child born since three of his other children had died.

With Hemda's help, the paper was thriving and Eliezer finally had time to organize the scraps of paper he'd been saving for years. He'd felt the need for a dictionary from the first day he had begun speaking Hebrew, but he never planned to write it himself. Maybe he had hoped that, once Hebrew began to be spoken, a language committee would spring up to organize the project. Few dictionaries are written by one person, the way a book is written. Many people work to create a dictionary.

Before Eliezer had a chance to think about how he would go about writing a dictionary, however, he found himself in serious trouble. Once again he had angered the Orthodox community and the Turkish authorities, but this time he was truly innocent. The problem began when Yonas,

Eliezer Ben-Yehuda's waist-high desk, at which he did much of his work for his paper, *Ha-Zvi*, as well as the dictionary

Hemda's father, who had come to visit, asked Eliezer if he could help him by running *Ha-Zvi*.

As Hanukkah approached, Father Yonas wanted to write something special. Hanukkah is an eight-day holiday which remembers the Maccabees' victory two thousand years ago and the Jewish people's return to Jewish life. *Ha-Zvi*'s main article was called "Good Deeds Require a Purpose." It reminded the pioneers of the courage and strength it took to rededicate their lives to Judaism in ancient times, and it encouraged the new citizens of the land to be like the Maccabees. The article said, "We must collect our forces and move forward."

Eliezer hadn't written the article, but he agreed with it. He also felt sure no one could find fault with his father-in-law's words. Everyone knew that settling a new land required bravery. But Eliezer was wrong. The Orthodox Jews took the words to mean that Jews should fight the Turks and win the land from them. This misunderstanding came from the language. The phrase *move forward* was an old Hebrew expression, *laassot hayil*. It usually meant "to progress," or "to go ahead," but it could also mean "to form an army."

The Orthodox community wanted to let the Turkish authorities know that they had nothing to do with Eliezer. They marched in the street with signs criticizing the article. Eliezer paid no attention until two Turkish policemen came to his house and took him to jail.

They put him in a damp, cold cell with ten other men, most of whom were in jail for murder. When Hemda came to see him, she wept. She didn't know what to do. They had no money to get him out of jail, and since the Orthodox community had put a ban on him again, even no Orthodox friend could help him. Eliezer might be imprisoned for a long time. If he wasn't sentenced to death, the jail might kill him because of his health.

The Turkish judges finally let him out of jail, eight days later, to wait for a future trial. He was happy to be home,

Edmond de Rothschild, who sent encouragement and monetary support to the struggling Ben-Yehuda in Palestine

but he wasn't free. He needed a lawyer to defend him, and he wasn't allowed to publish the paper. Having no money and being forced to be quiet was a different kind of prison.

For eight long months Palestine had no Hebrew newspaper. One of the conditions of his release was that he wouldn't publish *Ha-Zvi* until the trial was settled. He also didn't know what the jury would decide. The only hope he had of winning the trial came from Baron Edmond de Rothschild, a French millionaire who had given great sums of money to settle Palestine. He valued Eliezer's work and didn't want to see it end. So he sent money to help in the trial and warned the Orthodox Jews, *"Exercez vos prières,"* which means "Exercise your prayers." In other words, they were to mind their own business.

Eliezer finally was free. The money Rothschild sent bribed the judge. There was no other way to keep Eliezer from returning to jail. Relieved as he was, Eliezer was angry that he wouldn't be allowed to publish *Ha-Zvi* for four more months. At least he no longer worried about finding time to work on the dictionary. The newspaper was his first love. Only this rule could get him to give it up for work on the dictionary.

Since his Paris days, Eliezer had been writing down words he thought were helpful for conversation. At first he kept these words in a small notebook a Parisian grocer had given him. Eliezer was supposed to use the notebook to keep track of money he owed the grocer. But instead he arranged the book alphabetically and translated the Hebrew words into French.

For many years, he didn't have little notebooks for his word searches. Paper was scarce in Palestine. Eliezer wrote on anything he could find; wedding invitations, bills, and grocery lists were covered with his tiny handwriting. When Solomon Schecter, the first president of the Jewish Theological Seminary in New York and a well-known scholar, visited Eliezer, he couldn't believe how disorganized Eliezer was. He suggested that Eliezer use three-by-five-inch note cards, one card for each word. The simple plan had never crossed Eliezer's mind. From that day on, the future author of the modern Hebrew dictionary followed the professor's advice.

Still, Eliezer didn't approach his new project with joy. He didn't have the patience of a scholar. He was more like a warrior whose battle was to get people to speak Hebrew. He would do anything for this to happen, even if it meant writing a dictionary. He would write, years later, in the introduction to the dictionary:

I must admit that for the work of a real dictionary of the Hebrew language I was not in the least prepared,

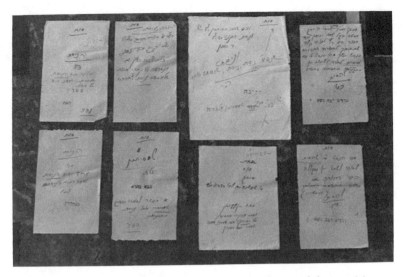

Some of the notes Ben-Yehuda prepared to aid his writing
of the dictionary   GAY BLOCK

not with respect to my knowledge of the science of language, and not with respect to my temperament. And
more than this: according to the spirit which prevailed
among the youth in Russia at that time, the science of
language, Philologie, was a little simple-minded in my
estimation, and I made fun of it. The study of language
was not a subject I enjoyed, and I had absolutely no
desire to become involved in it.

He became involved more than he had ever imagined. He
read thousands of books, cataloged twenty thousand more
books, and copied five hundred thousand references to Hebrew words. The dictionary would be the most gigantic work
in Hebrew literature since the Talmud. Its author, working
eighteen or nineteen hours a day, couldn't know how valu-
able his work would someday be. He described the work of
a compiler of words as hell. Over and over he would com-
plain of the work, tell anyone who would listen that it
was "not the work of one man." Those who listened to Eliezer had sympathy, but no one doubted that if anyone could

Above, Eliezer Ben-Yehuda at work among some of his books
ZIONIST ARCHIVES AND LIBRARY; *below,* this wall full of books
shows only a fraction of the number Ben-Yehuda utilized in
writing his Hebrew dictionary.   GAY BLOCK

do the job, it was he. Miracles seemed to be part of his life. His simply being alive amazed everyone, including his doctors. The dictionary would be one more miracle.

When Eliezer felt like an explorer and an inventor, he enjoyed the work. Inventing a new word from an ancient source was fun. He found the word for electricity from the word the Torah uses to describe the light Isaac saw in the sky. The word for garage came from part of Solomon's palace. Another example came from the story of Joseph. When Joseph first sees his brothers who had left him to die when he was a boy, he weeps. He possesses great power in the Pharaoh's court and can punish his brothers, yet when he sees how concerned they are for his father, his anger melts. He greets them with *"Avrekh!"* This can simply mean "I bless thee," or as the Talmud explains, it can be divided into *av*, "father," and *rakh*, "weak and little in years." Joseph had always been wise beyond his years. Based on this Talmudic suggestion, Eliezer defined *avrekh* as a young person who excels in scholarly achievements.

One of the first words he invented was a name for his book. *Dictionary* didn't exist in Hebrew. Eliezer used *milah*, which means "word," to create the word *milon* for dictionary. He also wanted to coin words that would be useful to children. A doll became *buba*, a bicycle became *offnayim*, and ice cream became *gelida*. Eliezer had found the word *gelida* used in the Talmudic commentaries of Rashi, a great Biblical scholar who lived in the first century C.E. (A.D.). The word may have come from early Hebrew, but it is like *gelato*, which is *ice cream* in Italian, and *gelidus*, which is *cold* in Latin, and Rashi may have borrowed it from European languages.

Not every new word was a success. In his efforts to make words from the ancient language, he sometimes came up with strange solutions. According to Eliezer, a phone was a *sakrahok*, a long distance conversation. Most people, however, liked the American name better and called it a telephone. His choice of words sometimes confused his chil-

Statue of Eliezer and Hemda Ben-Yehuda's children Ehud and Devorah   GAY BLOCK

dren. One day, when they returned home from the gym-nasia, their school, he told them that they would no longer be going there. The children were outraged. They de-manded to know why they couldn't return to it. Eliezer smiled and the children grew more puzzled. They rarely saw their father being playful. He explained to them that they would now attend the *midrasha*, which was his new word for high school, in place of gymnasia.

While Eliezer worked hard on his words, as he called them, Hemda began working on *Ha-Zvi* again once the ban had been lifted. The pioneers were starved for the paper and couldn't wait to read the new edition. In its first months, Eliezer and Hemda sold more copies than they had ever sold before. The extra money came in handy not only for their growing family—Ehud had been born less than a year after Devorah—but also for the dictionary.

The paper's success gave Eliezer enough money to pub-lish a forty-page dictionary in 1897. Although it was printed

Theodor Herzl on a boat bound for Palestine. The boat here is much like the vessel on which Eliezer and Devorah Ben-Yehuda traveled to Palestine. ZIONIST ARCHIVES AND LIBRARY

on brittle yellow paper and bound cheaply, it was one of the most important books in Jewish history. Eliezer found it the handsomest he'd ever seen. "Look," he'd say proudly, "this is the first real Hebrew dictionary in two thousand years." Every copy of the *milon* sold almost at once. Now Eliezer knew that the revival of Hebrew needed more than a newspaper; it needed a full-scale dictionary. The most important work he could do would be to expand the dictionary. He thought it would be complete with one thousand pages, but if he had had a crystal ball and could see how many pages and how many years it would actually take to complete his dictionary, he might never have attempted it. When completed, the entire work would include one hundred thousand words.

In 1897, Theodor Herzl, a young Hungarian journalist, organized the first World Zionist Congress in Basle, Switzerland. Eliezer was beginning to feel that the world was catching up to him. He longed to meet Herzl and attend the congress, but he knew the Turkish government would never let him go. They hated the idea of Zionism, because they wanted to continue to rule Palestine.

In his book *Der Judenstaat (The Jewish State)*, Herzl had made so powerful a case for a Jewish homeland that he would be remembered as the father of the Zionist movement even though he never lived in Palestine. He didn't say anything that Eliezer hadn't written sixteen years before, but he became famous for two reasons. First, by the end of the nineteenth century more Jews were ready to become Zionists. Second, he was a better writer. His words, "If you will it, it is no dream," became the Zionist slogan for fifty years. His writings moved a whole generation of Jews to do more than dream and pray. They got people to act.

To Eliezer's disappointment, Herzl didn't believe the country should have its own language. "Let the Jews go to Palestine and live there for a few generations," Herzl suggested. "After that they will decide themselves what language they wish to speak."

If Herzl had lived in Palestine, he might have changed his mind. The Jewish people needed all the help they could get to make the dream of a homeland real. The Zionist congress introduced a national anthem, written in Hebrew, for the unborn country. It was called "Hatikvah" ("The Hope"). The congress also proudly displayed a blue and white flag for the time when the hope became reality. In the meantime, the Jewish people had a common language to make them feel united. Until they had a place to fly their flag and sing their song, Hebrew would substitute for a homeland.

EIGHT

The War of Words

Eliezer had had grand plans for seventeen-year-old Ben Zion. He had arranged for his son to go to Paris and study at the Ecole Normal. "No, I won't," said Ben Zion to his father. He was in love with a young woman from Jerusalem and didn't want to leave her. He'd made enough sacrifices being Eliezer Ben-Yehuda's son. Eliezer couldn't understand this. The rebirth of spoken Hebrew was his life. Everything else had to fit into this goal. How could his son choose love instead of a fine education? Only when Eliezer explained to Ben Zion how important it was for the world to see that a person with a purely Hebrew education knows enough to attend a European university did Ben Zion give in and agree to go to France.

Soon after arriving in Paris, Ben Zion, like his father, changed his name. He took the name his parents originally

Eliezer Ben-Yehuda with his wife Hemda and son Ben Zion

wanted for him, Ittamar. He also changed his last name to Ben-Avi, which means son of the father.

Five years after her stepson, in 1904, Hemda also left for Europe. The dictionary was going to be much longer than the thousand pages Eliezer had originally thought. In fact, it would have to be published in separate volumes, one at a time. The first volume alone would be several hundred pages. The more Eliezer worked, the more he worried. "How will I ever get this published?" he asked Hemda. "I don't have the money to get a book this size printed."

So Hemda, always resourceful, went to Europe to speak to wealthy European Jews about her husband's work. She took with her the heavy manuscript of the first volume. Eliezer had set the first word himself with his printer's typesetting equipment. Appropriately enough, it was *av*, which means "father." Everyone was interested and enthusiastic about the work, but they asked, "Why is it so long?" After all, the Torah has only 7,704 words. The reason for the book's length was that Eliezer had written more than a dictionary. He'd written an encyclopedia and history of the Jewish people. He'd done this by including all the Hebrew words used from the time the language was first spoken. His definitions gave pictures of life at home, in schools, in Europe. Eliezer was interested in more than nouns and verbs. He was interested in how words were used by people in ancient times and how they could be used in the modern world.

Every defined word was translated into French, German, and English. He didn't only define words, but he also provided synonyms, the way a thesaurus would, for each word. He also wanted to show all the different meanings a word could have. For example, the dictionary offered 335 expressions for the word *lo*, which means "no," and 210 for *ken*, which means "yes."

Hemda wrote Eliezer that she was getting plenty of money to publish the first volume, but he only half believed her. He wanted so much for her words to be true, yet he was afraid she exaggerated her success to make him feel better. He feared she did it only to put his mind at ease.

When she returned four months later, she carried home the dummy, or model, of the first volume of his dictionary. It was printed on the thin, crisp paper used for the world's great dictionaries and it was bound in leather. Gold letters on the front read:

Thesaurus Totius Hebraitatis
et Veteris et Recentioris
Auctore Elieser Ben-Jehuda
Hierosolymitano

A Complete Dictionary of Ancient and Modern Hebrew, by Eliezer Ben-Yehuda of Jerusalem. The words were in Latin because

אל הספרייה ע"ש אריה (סיר ליאון) סיימון

Sign pointing to the Academy of the Hebrew Language—the
institution created by Ben-Yehuda to expand and enrich Hebrew GAY BLOCK

Latin is the language of scholars. Willingly or unwillingly,
Eliezer had joined the ranks of language scientists.

Satisfied as he was with his first volume, he knew it was
just the beginning. "If I am privileged to write the last word
in the dictionary," he wrote, "then I will need the aid of
heaven to keep my heart from breaking under the emo-
tion."

Soon after the first volume was printed, Eliezer created
the Vaad ha-Lashon ha-Ivrit, "Hebrew Language Council,"
to help him revive old words and create new ones. He'd
been doing this for over twenty years, but there was still
much to be done. The Hebrew Language Council would
expand Hebrew into a conversational language that included scientific and technical terms.

Not everyone believed that Hebrew could make the leap

into the twentieth century. Many European Jews were proud of their tradition but felt very much like citizens of the countries in which they lived. This was especially true of German Jews. They supported settlements in Palestine but expected the people to speak German or Yiddish. In 1913, the German-speaking Hilfsverein settlement planned to build the first college in Palestine. Built in Haifa, it would be a technological school that would teach the most up-to-date scientific ideas. The money for the college came from Jews all over the world.

When the building was almost finished, the Jews in Palestine were proud and happy, including one of the earliest pioneers, Eliezer Ben-Yehuda. The good feelings about the school vanished, however, when the members of the school's board of directors who were from the Hilfsverein settlement made it clear that they planned to have the classes conducted in German. This was a serious step backward.

Eliezer had convinced teachers all over Palestine, except in the Orthodox community, to teach all subjects in Hebrew. One of the main reasons Hebrew was beginning to be spoken everywhere was that children learned it in school and brought it home to their parents. For such an important school to be taught in German was a slap in the face of everyone who had worked to make Hebrew the language of Palestine. The protest astounded the German board members. They were sure the settlers would understand their decision. German was a modern language from a country known for its scientific interest. "Chemistry and physics cannot be taught in an ancient language," they said flatly. Oddly enough, they wanted to call the school the Technicum, which was a Latin name.

When the teachers in Palestine discovered that the board had chosen a German director of the school who knew no Hebrew, they told the board that Hebrew would be the language of the school or they wouldn't teach. Even the teachers in the Hilfsverein refused to teach in protest against the college. The entire community of settlers helped the cause.

Young children refused to go to the Hilfsverein schools. Some burned their textbooks and chanted, "We shall never need German schoolbooks again!"

American Jews had given a large amount of money for the Technicum. They didn't want German to be the language of instruction, either. Most believed that Hebrew ought to be its language. Because of this feeling, the American members of the Technicum's board convinced the German members to drop their plan. On February 22, 1914, the board met and decided that mathematics and physics be taught in Hebrew immediately. For the other subjects, the board allowed teachers four years to either learn or create the vocabulary necessary for teaching in Hebrew.

Sometimes an event happens and everyone alive at the time senses that history will record that moment as important. The signing of the Declaration of Independence was that kind of event. Other events, however, don't seem so important at the time but make a great difference later on. The invention of the first car is an example. When the Technicum (a Latin word), renamed the Technion (a Hebrew word), chose Hebrew as its language of instruction, it was more than a momentary victory for Eliezer and his followers.

Hebrew had earned a new respect. There would never again be a question of what language to use in the schools. Hebrew had already proven itself in the home, among children, and in the workplace. Now it would be used to express sophisticated modern thought in the university. The War of Language, as it was called, was the first real test of whether Hebrew would be accepted as a living language. The Technion's decision helped Hebrew once again to be the language of the Jewish people.

N I N E

"My Work Is Blessed"

By 1917, Eliezer had a new sign over his desk. The message proclaimed:

MY DAY IS LONG
MY WORK IS BLESSED

He was sixty years old. No one, especially Eliezer, would have believed that he could live that long. Since the time he knew that he had a fatal disease, he had fathered eleven children, had published the first modern newspaper in Palestine, had written five tremendous volumes of the Hebrew dictionary, had created thousands of new Hebrew words, and had led the struggle to revive Hebrew as a spoken language. These were accomplishments enough for anyone.

That Eliezer had been able to change his work motto was important. One of his great strengths was the passion he gave to his work. But passionate people are rarely patient, especially if they believe their lives will be short. Yet the revival of Hebrew was a slow process. It wasn't as though King Eliezer could come to the land of Palestine and say to its Jewish population, "From this day hence, everyone will speak Hebrew!" Even if everyone thought speaking Hebrew again was a fine idea, it couldn't happen overnight. It takes people time to learn a language, and if the language hasn't been used for two thousand years, it takes even more time.

When Eliezer first walked the streets of Jerusalem, he heard people speaking Arabic, Yiddish, Ladino, Hebrew, and a variety of European languages. The Jewish people had no language of their own. Almost forty years later, thirty-four thousand people spoke Hebrew as their first or only language. This was almost all Eliezer's doing, but forty years was a long time for an impatient man to wait. Still, he was lucky he lived to see his dream come true. Hebrew had been declared the language of Palestine, along with Arabic and English.

He knew, however, that Hebrew wasn't enough to revive the spirit of the Jewish people. The land was equally important. Since Herzl's death in 1904, there had been little progress in making Palestine the Jewish homeland.

But on November 2, 1917, the British government declared: "His Majesty's Government views with favor the establishment in Palestine of a national home for the Jewish people." The document was called the Balfour Declaration, but Eliezer had another name for it. He called it "our charter of freedom." The Jews in Palestine danced in the streets to celebrate coming closer to their dream. Even though nothing had changed in Palestine, the Balfour Declaration made things different. They still didn't have a country, but the Jewish people felt that they had returned home.

It was good that Eliezer was beginning to see his dreams come true, because his illness was finally beginning to beat

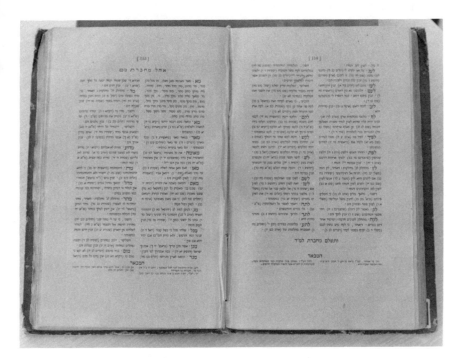

Two pages from Ben-Yehuda's masterpiece—the Hebrew
dictionary   GAY BLOCK

him. He coughed constantly, and each bloody cough fur-
ther weakened him. He'd written five volumes of the dictionary, and he wasn't half-finished. He began to make notes
and plans for the rest of the dictionary. When it was finally
completed in 1959, by his son Ehud and Hemda, it was a
sixteen-volume dictionary.

Hemda tried to create a perfect little world for her husband in which to work. She gave him only good news and
edited out the bad. But this didn't last long. Good journalist
that he was, Eliezer always knew when trouble was around,
and if he could help, he'd be there.

Since the Balfour Declaration, there had been many battles between the Arabs and the Jews. The British weren't
doing much to make peace. Besides causing fear and suffering among the people in Palestine, the wars were also keep-

ing European Jews from coming to Palestine. Much as they hated their treatment in Russia and Poland, they were more afraid of the Arabs and British soldiers.

In 1922, Chaim Weizmann, a brilliant young man, led the Zionists. He was one of the few Zionists who was liked and respected by both the British and the settlers. He needed Eliezer's help, and even though Weizmann knew how ill Eliezer was, he had to ask him. Weizmann knew how many Jews Eliezer had brought to Palestine through his writings.

He asked Eliezer for one more appeal to Jews all over the world. The Jewish people outside Israel were just beginning to think of Palestine as a Jewish homeland. Someone had to convince them that it needed the loyalty of all Jews. Eliezer said, "What can I write that will be better than the Balfour Declaration? If that didn't convince them, what can I say?" Weizmann persisted and, in the end, Eliezer agreed to write the appeal.

But for once his will failed. For three nights he tried to write, but the ideas wouldn't come. Hemda saw him struggling on the third night near midnight and took the pen from his hand. He told her that he wasn't going to be able to finish his work. Two hours later, on the first night of Hanukkah, he was dead.

If Eliezer could have been at his own funeral, he might have been amused. In life he had fought with different groups—he never would have won a popularity contest. But finally Eliezer was appreciated. Thirty thousand people came to his funeral. The government declared three days of national mourning. He was buried near Devorah and his children, at the Mount of Olives.

Eliezer's popularity and influence grew after his death. He became a national hero. Ben-Yehuda Streets are prominent in Tel Aviv and Jerusalem. Three million people in Israel speak Hebrew as their native language. The language continues to change and grow richer. American TV shows such as "Dallas" and "The A-Team" are given lively translations on Israeli television. And Hebrew novels are translated around the world. Once it was the other way around.

One hundred years ago no one outside of Palestine spoke Hebrew. Some people told Eliezer Ben-Yehuda that it couldn't be done; others told him it shouldn't be done. He didn't listen. Instead, he reunited the Jewish people with their ancient language and at the same time gave them a voice in the modern world. They had a modern language which fit the times but also connected them to their beginnings. It became a spoken language again, and gave the Jewish people a way to express themselves as Jews in the modern world.

The last word he worked on in the dictionary was *nefesh*, which means "soul" or "spirit." In the Jewish tradition, this is the part of a person that makes him or her unique. It is also the part that connects that person to God and exists forever. The *nefesh* in Eliezer Ben-Yehuda gave his body strength to survive long enough to revive the language the Jewish people believe God spoke to create the world.

Index

Page numbers in *italics* refer to captions.

About the Author

Malka Drucker is a veteran writer in the area of Jewish culture. She has written the Jewish Holidays series, of which the Jewish Book Council said, "Each new book by Malka Drucker is a time to rejoice." This series won the Award for Excellence in a Series, given by the Southern California Council on Literature for Children and Young People. Three of her books have been nominees for the National Jewish Book Award. Ms. Drucker has also written two other biographies and a book on how a television show is made.

Of this book she says, "Eliezer Ben-Yehuda and his family sacrificed and suffered for the creation of modern Hebrew. My recent visit to Israel, as a student of the language, helped me see how alive and expressive Hebrew is."

Ms. Drucker lives in Los Angeles, California.